To Judy
Happy Christmas
2018
Lots of love from
Malcolm, Alison
& All The Gang.

xxp

Who Was Betty?

When I launched my Rainforest Project in 2007 one of the very first people to offer their support was Jonathan Wild of Bettys & Taylors of Harrogate. In the years that have followed, he has shown an unwavering passion for this crucial subject and I am delighted to be able to contribute a short foreword to this charming book, "Who was Betty?".

Quite simply, if we are to stand any chance of maintaining a stable environment for future generations, then we have to preserve the rainforests. Not only are they home to a dizzying array of biodiversity, including millions of species which are still unknown to Man, they are also the source of much of the rainfall which is so essential for agriculture around the world. Not only that, but their desperately important role as a carbon store means they are on the frontline in the battle to combat catastrophic climate change. To preserve an area of rainforest the size of Yorkshire is an important step and, as someone who loves and admires both Bettys and Harrogate, I can only congratulate most warmly Jonathan and everyone involved for the excellent work they are doing.

First published in Great Britain in 2011 by Bettys & Taylors Group,
1 Parliament Street, Harrogate, HG1 2QU

We thank the contributors to *Who Was Betty?* for giving us
permission to use their work in our collection. Copyright for
individual works remains with the respective contributors.

Introduction by Jonathan Wild

Edited by Sam Gibson

Designed by Laura Jukes and Rebecca Watson

Printed by Team (Impression) Limited, Leeds

ISBN 978-0-9550914-3-8

Contents

Introduction

Take it from me – and I should know – Betty's identity is *not* a family secret.

Not one living member of our family knows for sure who the mysterious 'Betty' was who provided the inspiration for our Great Uncle Fritz 'Frederick' Belmont's tea room business.

There are plenty of clues, of course, and Uncle Frederick must be tickled pink in his grave at the thought that we are still puzzling over his romantic secret a hundred years later.

Yes, Uncle Frederick was a great one for 'tickling' the ladies, and in the years before his marriage to our Auntie Bunny in 1916, when he was a young journeyman confectioner and chocolatier plying his trade all over Yorkshire, he certainly 'tickled' a fair few pretty girls.

And we have his postcard collection from that time to prove it. Yes, postcards were the texts and emails of the day, the way of making and confirming assignations, written in the morning and delivered that same afternoon.

But there's not a message from a 'Betty' amongst them.

Not to worry, our family is well known for its fertile imagination, and over the years we have put two and two together and come up with a number of theories, one of which I reveal for the first time in this little book.

But now that a hundred years have passed it feels like an appropriate moment to let some of Yorkshire's finest and most famous imaginations loose on the mystery of 'Who Was Betty?'

It's a bit of fun. And more than that. These authors are doing it to help us raise funds for our 'Yorkshire Rainforest Project', an ambitious Bettys & Taylors project which aims to support the conservation of tropical rainforests the size of our old county of Yorkshire.

It's a cause that would have tickled Uncle Frederick.

After pretty girls and fine chocolate – and perhaps a good whisky – he loved the natural world of our planet, and at night, whisky glass in one hand, he would marvel at the wonders of the heavens above through a powerful brass telescope.

My brother, sister and I inherited that marvellous telescope and played with it for hours as children.

I always thought that it was the kind of telescope that a pirate captain would use. Maybe it was...

And so, to all our contributors and their imaginations, a big 'thank you'.

And to you the reader, as you delve into the mystery of Betty, imagine way beyond the reach of Uncle's telescope the wondrous biodiversity of the 'Yorkshire' rainforest you are helping to conserve for future generations, and take pride and comfort in your contribution.

Jonathan Wild

From the 'Bettys' founding family

'...'Scuse me miss, are you Betty?'

JONATHAN WILD

A Drop or Two of Pirate Blood

A letter from Jonathan Wild, a 'Bettys' founding family
member, to his young grandson 'D'.

April 7th 2011

My Dearest Grandson 'D',

I must have been about your age – five or six years
old – when my mother first whispered in my ear that I
had 'a drop or two of pirate blood' in me.

She even gave me a pirate name – 'Little Rascal' –
which she only ever used in private. I was extremely

proud of it and ached to tell my school friends.

'It's our little secret,' she used to say. 'Don't ever tell anyone. Not even your father. Not ever.'

'Not ever, ever, ever?' I asked, tears of frustration in my eyes.

'Well, not for fifty years, anyway,' she said, offering some hope.

Fifty years didn't sound like a concession to me. Fifty years to a five year old is as good as forever.

I don't know where those fifty years went, but here I am, fifty-six years old and ready to tell the truth. Yes, the family that founded and still owns Bettys is descended from pirates! And that means you too, grandson.

'But aren't we a Swiss family?' you may ask. 'Surely there are no Swiss pirates? Switzerland is land-locked: there's no "High Seas" to roam around looking for treasure islands or ships laden with Spanish gold to plunder. Go on, pull the other one!'

Hah! 'Pulling the other one' – that's a cruel pirate joke of course, told by one-legged pirates as their prisoners begged for mercy. 'Mercy?' they would say, drawing their cutlasses, 'Pull the other one!'

Look, take it from me 'D' – and I should know – there are Swiss pirates, and one of our long-dead relatives, Fritz – the one who started Bettys – was one of them.

Orphaned at the age of five, Fritz was snatched from his Geneva orphanage in the dead of night by a pirate captain and trained as one of his 'powder monkeys' – the small boys who crawl around below deck fetching and carrying gunpowder and loading the cannons.

The Great Swiss Lake of Geneva is big enough to be considered as one of the 'High Seas' and Fritz's captain – 'Two Hooks Toulon' – was the most feared pirate who sailed upon it.

The most feared? Well only until the day that Fritz, now a bold nineteen-year-old cut-throat who went by the name of 'Fingers' Fritz, threw Captain 'Two Hooks Toulon' overboard and took command of the pirate ship himself.

Now the first thing a new pirate captain has to do is to register his new name with the Nominations Committee of the Worldwide Pirate Captains' Association, the W.P.C.A.

'Fingers' is a fine name for a pirate, and it well described Fritz's long, strong pincer-like fingers, but there are plenty of pirates called 'Fingers'. No, a pirate captain must adopt a name and a flag that is unique to him and have it approved by the Committee. They decide whether the captain is worthy of the new name and check that no other captain on the register has that name.

The Nominations Committee meet once a year, on the first day of the pirates' W.P.C.A. Conference, a five-day event at which pirate captains discuss the very latest in hooks, peg-legs and eye patches, sell and buy treasure maps, stock up on cannon balls and that sort of thing. Pirates aren't usually a friendly, sociable lot, so a United Nations Peacekeeping Force is hired to maintain the ceasefire for the five days of the conference.

Now that year – nineteen hundred and six – the annual pirate captains' conference was to be held in the Yorkshire seaport of Whitby.

'Fingers' Fritz couldn't sail to Whitby, as most captains did, because the Great Swiss Lake of Geneva is completely land-locked. So, he disguised himself as a 'landlubber' and travelled by train all the way from Switzerland to Yorkshire.

Arriving in Whitby in the early evening he changed into his freshly washed and pressed pirate captain's uniform and made an appointment to see the Nominations Committee the following morning. Fingers crossed, by this time tomorrow he would be known as Captain 'Little Rascal' and his flag – 'the skull and crossed alphorns' – approved. Surely the Committee couldn't turn him down? After all he was 'Little' – barely five foot five tall – and certainly a 'Rascal'. I mean, a nineteen-year-old pirate who tosses his captain overboard and seizes his ship couldn't be called anything else.

Little in stature 'Fingers' Fritz may have been, but he cut a fine figure that evening as he strolled out of Whitby town along the lane that led to the cliffs.

The buttons on his captain's jacket sparkled in the moonlight, as did his handsome pale face, which unusually for a pirate was not battle-scarred at all. Not only that, all his limbs were present and correct. No peg-leg, no hook at the end of his arm, no eye patch over a missing eye. Yes, 'Fingers' Fritz still had two of everything. Except half the middle finger of his left hand was missing, blown off when a cannon misfired while he was still a seven-year-old 'powder monkey'.

He passed the sheds where fishermen hang raw fish over smouldering oak fires and turn them into 'kippers', the oily smoked fish that anyone with a drop or two of pirate blood in them – like you – loves to eat for breakfast.

Just at that moment one of the shed doors flew open and a cloud of smoke came billowing out and engulfed 'Fingers' Fritz. He heard an angry voice shouting 'What are you doing hiding in my shed, laddie? Out to steal my fish, eh? I'll cut your throat for that!'

And then suddenly something smacked into 'Fingers' Fritz's chest and almost knocked him over. The something was a someone, a small lad by the feel of him. 'Fingers' Fritz grasped him by the collar and carried him off, away from the smoke and towards the cliffs.

The lad kicked and squealed. 'Don't worry, lad,' said 'Fingers' Fritz, 'I'm not going to hurt you. I'm not armed to the teeth. I'm a pirate captain come to the conference. I had to hand in all my weapons to the United Nations Peacekeeping soldiers at the town gates.' And he let go of the lad, stood back and looked at him in the moonlight. He was covered in black soot and stank like a fish. But he could just make out the colour of the lad's head wear: white. A white headscarf! The white headscarf worn by all pirate ships' cooks to make sure they didn't get their throats cut if they were captured. A good ship's cook was as valuable as a treasure chest, so they were always spared the bloody fate of the rest of a captured crew.

'You're a cook, aren't you lad?'

'Yes sir, I am a pirate ship's cook. From the *Bloody Mary*.'

'So you were stealing some kippers for your crew's breakfast tomorrow?'

'No sir, I was hiding. I was running away.'

'Running away from what, my young lad?'

'I've been "swopped" for a treasure map. My captain has put me in the clutches of the cruellest, ugliest, foulest pirate captain in the world – "The Madraggon" – and he doesn't just want a cook, he wants a wife! "The Madraggon's" going to force me to marry him tomorrow!'

'Marry you? But you're a boy!' and saying that
'Fingers' Fritz took out a handkerchief and wiped the
soot off the lad's face.

It was the most beautiful face of the most beautiful
girl he had ever seen. He looked at her. She looked at
him. Hearts fluttered. Yes, it was love at first sight!

He took her in his arms and whispered: 'Dearest
girl, what's your name?'

'Betty. And what's yours, captain?'

'"Fingers". No that's my old name. I'm going to
become Captain "Little Rascal" tomorrow.'

'Tomorrow? But I can't stay here tonight. "The
Madraggon" will be after me. My only hope is to run
away inland. I have an aunt – Auntie Jessie – who lives
three days' walk away, over the wild moors. But I'm
so afraid to go on the moors at night, all on my own.
That's why I was hiding in that shed full of smoking
fish.'

'Don't worry, I'll come with you Betty,' said
'Fingers' Fritz.

'But what about your ship? What about becoming

Captain "Little Rascal" tomorrow?!'

'I don't care about any of that any more,' said 'Fingers' Fritz, 'I only care about you! Piracy is going to be a thing of the past soon. Our old fashioned sailing ships can't keep up with these modern steamships. Mark my words, in ten years' time there won't be a real pirate ship left on the "High Seas". No, good riddance to all that. I'm coming with you. By the way, no need to call me "Fingers" or "Captain Rascal". Just call me Fritz. I am yours for ever, dearest, dearest Betty.'

So that's that 'D'. The end of a pirate story. But the beginning of a love-story, which I know is a bit soppy, but you need to hear it, because it explains why you and I both have a drop or two of pirate blood in us. I'll write it all down in another letter and send it to you next week.

Your loving Grandad

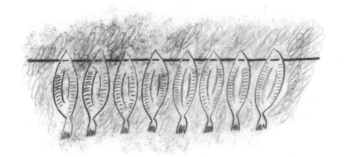

My Dearest Grandson 'D',

Betty's Auntie Jessie lived in a cottage by the River Ouse, a few miles north of the City of York.

The River Ouse was busy with traffic: boats of all kinds carrying grain, wool, coal and so on for sale in the markets of York. Betty thought it would be a good idea to use her wonderful cooking skills by opening a baker's shop on the banks of the river.

Fritz was finding it hard to settle down. True, he now had the most wonderful wife in the world, but he was missing the pirate life. He built a look-out – a 'crow's nest' – in a tree overlooking the river and hung his black-and-white 'skull and crossed alphorns' flag from a branch. And he closed his eyes and imagined he could see an enemy ship on the horizon. 'Powder monkeys' to your stations! Load the cannon!' he yelled.

'I'll "powder monkey" you in a moment if you don't come down from that tree and give me a hand with the baking!' shouted Betty.

It didn't sound like shouting to Fritz. It sounded like a sweet melody played on a flute. By a princess. His princess.

He scrambled down the tree like a monkey and followed Betty into the bakery.

'Just decorate those buns for me please,' said Betty. 'Use some bits of dried fruit and nuts and make the shape of a little flower.'

Fritz started to decorate the buns. His mind wandered back to his days of pirate adventures. 'Hoist the "skull and crossed alphorns" and prepare for battle!' a voice in his head cried.

'Darling what have you done?' exclaimed Betty. 'Those aren't pretty flowers! You've gone and decorated those buns with the skull from your pirate flag!'

Fritz looked down at his handiwork. Sure enough, every bun was staring back at him like a terrifying skull. A red cherry for each eye and three almonds for the teeth.

'Now do the rest like flowers, dearest,' said Betty exasperated. 'I don't know. We can't afford to throw the "skulls" away; we'll just have to put them on sale next to the buns with flowers.'

Well, of course, you can guess, can't you 'D'? The skulls sold first. So they made some more. And more. And more.

'Well dearest,' said Betty. 'I give up. The pirate skull wins, but you'll have to make them every day yourself. You can dream of the pirate life while you're making them. In fact, I'm going to call them after you. From now on we're going to call those skulls "Captain Rascals".'

Betty and Fritz were both very happy. Especially when their baby came along. A beautiful little girl. They called her Kate.

And then.......

And then. And then Betty died. She was only twenty three years old, but they had some horrible diseases a hundred years ago that no one had a cure for.

Fritz was convinced that the loathsome pirate captain 'The Madraggon' had tracked them down and poisoned Betty out of revenge. But he couldn't prove it.

Fritz was heartbroken. He couldn't bear to stay living by the river where he had been so happy with his Betty, so he left baby Kate in the care of Aunt Jessie, and set off to find fame and fortune in another part of Yorkshire.

All he took with him were his pirate captain's

uniform, his pirate flag, the recipe for 'Captain Rascals' and his beloved dead wife's white cook's headscarf. And a head full of memories. Memories of those pirate days, memories of his dearest Betty, and memories of little Kate who he had left behind.

Fritz settled in a very smart town called Harrogate, and opened a little baker's shop and café.

The 'Captain Rascals' sold by the hundreds and thousands but the café was even more popular. Especially with the ladies. You see, Fritz stood at the door welcoming customers wearing his best pirate captain's uniform. He looked so handsome that ladies came to the café just to admire him.

One day a very smart lady brought in her seventeen-year-old daughter, Bunny, to show her 'the pirate captain and his Rascals'. The daughter felt the sleeve of his pirate jacket, then looked into his eyes and said: 'I think you really are a pirate captain!'

'Don't be silly, darling,' said the mother. 'He just dresses up to attract the customers. It's just a gimmick; he's not really a pirate.'

But it was too late. The pirate captain and Bunny had, in that moment, fallen headlong in love.

They married and worked together running the bakery and café. It was very successful, and they opened more cafés in other Yorkshire towns.

'Darling, you've never told me why you call it Bettys Café,' said Bunny one day.

Fritz had never told his new wife the truth about his pirate past, or about his first love, Betty, or even about baby Kate. That was all in the past. He was a respectable businessman now. Skeletons – especially pirate skeletons – in his cupboard had to stay there, hidden. It would cause a scandal if customers found out the truth about his past.

'Oh, you know darling. This and that. I can't really remember why I called it "Bettys". It can't have been anyone important. Probably someone from my day as a Swiss pira... – I mean baker.'

The years passed. Fritz and Bunny were very happy, but very tired. They didn't have any children to help them in the bakery or the cafés, and they were getting busier and busier.

'I know,' said Fritz one day. 'My Swiss sister has a son, a young man called Viktor. I'll ask if he'll come over and help us at Bettys.'

Young Viktor arrived and was very, very good at baking, and at charming the customers in the cafés.

'One day, Viktor, all these cafés will be yours,' said Fritz, 'but now I'd like to take you to meet Auntie Jessie. She lives by a river. It will be a nice run out in the car. But don't tell Bunny where we are going. It's a bit of a secret. By the way, Auntie Jessie has a teenage daughter called Kate. It's funny but Kate likes to call me "daddy". She's very pretty; you'll like her.'

Like her? No sooner had Viktor and Kate set eyes on each other than they fell in love.

They married a few months later. Fritz couldn't have been happier. His beloved but secret daughter, Kate, was one of the family again.

And then Viktor and Kate had a baby. And it was me! Yes, 'D', I am Kate and Viktor's son. So, as Kate's parents were Fritz and Betty, that means my grandfather was a Swiss pirate and my grandmother was a pirate ship's cook. Now that's more than a drop or two of pirate blood, isn't it?

And it means, 'D', that your great-great-grandparents were pirates, one called 'Fingers' Fritz and one called 'Betty'. How cool is that?

So next time you bite into a Bettys 'Rascal' bun, remember you are biting into a piece of blood-thirsty pirate history.

And if you ever hear the name 'Madraggon', I would 'hoist the mainsail' and get out of here very, very fast. You don't want to mess with pirates.

So now you know our family secret, grandson, and why I call you 'D' when there are other people around. And why when we are alone I call you by your inherited pirate captain's name: 'Little Rascal'.

But from now on, I don't mind you telling your friends about your pirate family. I expect no-one will believe you.

You and I know the truth, and that's what's really important.

Your loving Grandad

ALAN AYCKBOURN

The truth is there was no such person as Betty. 'Betty' was dreamt up by the Tea Room's first public relations officer in 1922, one Josiah Candlewick, who created the mnemonic Best Ever Tasty Teas Yet which, because of lack of space on the café's original frontage, was immediately shortened to B E T T Y. This became colloquially known as Bettys and so finally, bowing to public pressure, the owners added the 's' to the signage (certainly more than Marks and Spencer ever did) which is how we know the much-loved Tea Rooms to this very day.

Alan Ayckbourn is one of the world's most popular playwrights with a prolific back catalogue of work, which has won countless awards and been performed in theatres around the world. The majority of his work has been premièred at the Stephen Joseph Theatre in Scarborough, where he was Artistic Director for 37 years. In 1997 he received a knighthood for services to theatre.

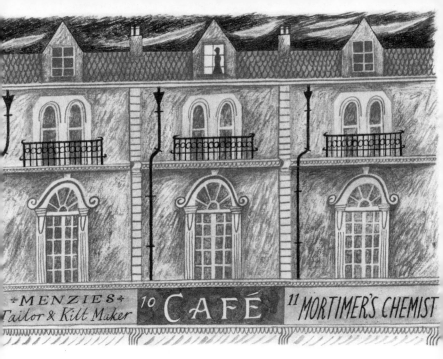

ANONYMOUS
The Apprentice

Betty was furious. What right did these people have to trespass on her property? After all, it was her home, wasn't it? Well she had lived there for over 80 years, so she had more of a right to it than anyone else, even though she didn't actually own it.

But that wasn't the point.

She was standing in the middle of the attic of number 10 Cambridge Crescent, which she had just been passing through on her way from the attic of number 9 to the attic of number 11. It was a regular routine that she enjoyed every evening; indeed she looked forward to it.

Number 9 Cambridge Crescent was occupied by Mr. Menzies, tailor and kilt maker, who owned the gentleman's outfitters on the ground floor. He used the attic as his storeroom, so it was piled high with boxes of every shape and size containing collars and studs, formal evening shirts, waistcoats for day or evening wear, fine silk cravats and cummerbunds for visits to the Kursaal theatre, kid gloves, silk socks and suspenders, moleskin trousers and sleek top hats. Not to mention the boxes of gentleman's unmentionables. Every evening Mr. Menzies, or one of his snooty assistants, came up to the attic to collect fresh stock to replace what they had sold during the day. Every evening Betty settled herself into a corner to watch as he nervously approached the shelves, list in hand, looking around to see if there was any sign of her presence. She could hardly contain herself with anticipation of the fright she was going to give him. She pushed a box right off the shelf behind him, scattering buttons and bow ties all over the floor. With a shriek he was off, galloping down the narrow attic stairs, complaining, 'It's happened again! That attic is haunted, I swear.'

After she had recovered from laughing at her trick on the tailor's assistant, she usually made her way through to the attic of number 11.

Number 11 Cambridge Crescent was rented by Mr. Mortimer, the chemist, who lived with his wife and three children above his shop. The children shared an attic bedroom, with three windows overlooking the gardens of the Prospect Hotel where Betty used to work as a chambermaid, before her life was brought to a premature end when a carriage overturned on top of her.

The children, William, Charles and Fanny, were usually in their beds, sleepy but not yet fully asleep. For some reason that she couldn't fathom, the children could see her perfectly well, and they weren't at all frightened of her. It was nice to sit on the edge of their bed and tell them stories she remembered from when she was their age, living in Prospect Cottage with her father. It made her feel warm and almost alive, which was a nice change to how she normally felt, a bit vague and blurry and not quite there.

But tonight, as she floated through the normally empty attic of number 10, she was stopped in her tracks by the sight of two burly workmen wrestling pieces of a large cast iron oven into place. In her attic. And that wasn't all. There was rubble in heaps everywhere and a large hole in the floor with a view of the room below. There were workmen in that room too, laying bricks and mixing plaster in big pails. She caught sight of a tall, rather distinguished-looking gentleman who seemed to be giving instructions to the workmen in a strange accent that she hadn't heard before. She thought he looked rather handsome with his elegant, sweeping moustache, but couldn't understand a word he was saying. Something about 'Mein Schweizer Café' and 'frich und zart'*. The workmen were deferential and tipped their caps when he left, saying, 'right you are Mr Belmont.'

Betty wasn't at all pleased about this disturbance and resolved to frighten them all away so that things could return to the nice, peaceful routine she was used to.

In the weeks that followed she tried several times

to disrupt the building works. Her first attempt went almost unnoticed. She emerged through a wall on one side and passed quite purposefully through a small man called Sidney who was painting the wall. She had intended that this would send a ghostly shiver through his bones, but instead he complained to his mate about a 'reet draught from yonder chimney' and the next day he came to work wearing a thick woollen scarf his wife had fashioned out of an old pair of trousers.

She then tried making objects fly through the air. Unfortunately Betty had never fully mastered this ghostly technique, so the best she could muster was causing Sidney's mug of tea to slide off the shelf into a bag containing the bread and cheese he had brought for his lunch, which made her feel rather ashamed of herself.

As the work progressed she found herself less concerned with inventing ways to scare the workmen away, and became fascinated by the comings and goings at number 10.

The rather dashing Frederick Belmont came several times a day to oversee the work and to supervise the installation of various items of machinery. First the cast iron oven, then a long marble-topped table and another with a wooden top, a strange mangle device, big mixing bowls, wooden rolling pins, and racks laden with sacks of flour, sugar, dried fruit and spices. The air became perfumed with an exotic aroma emanating from huge slabs of chocolate.

A wooden cabinet was erected over the hole in the floor, containing a box connected to a rope pulley that could be pulled to allow the box to move between floors. Mr. Belmont called it a 'dumb waiter'.

While he was testing the dumb waiter, Betty slipped inside and when she slipped out again two floors below, she found herself in a beautiful dining room with muted pink walls edged in old silver gilt, lit by lamps that looked like candles, but the workman called 'lectric'. A gaggle of young girls about the same age as herself were being critically inspected by an elegantly dressed woman, whom Frederick addressed as Bunny, but the girls called Mrs. Belmont. She made them line up in order of height and went along the line checking to see if their hands were clean, their nails short and neat, their white aprons uncrumpled with perfectly tied bows, and no stray hairs escaping from their starched headdresses. Betty thought they looked very smart and stylish, and their uniforms were much more elegant than the unflattering black skirt, stiff white blouse and linen cuffs she had to wear at The Prospect.

On the ground floor, carpenters and glaziers were putting the finishing touches to the shop fittings. The polished wood gleamed, reflected in the mirrored walls, and row after row of empty glass shelves waited expectantly to be filled with tantalising fancies with names like Sarah Bernhardt and Chocolate Leopold. One of the workmen was perched at the top of a tall ladder painting gold letters along the top of a glass cabinet. Betty wasn't particularly good at reading, because she'd left school when she was 11 to go into service, but she did recognise these words because she had seen them before in Standings grocery shop on James Street. It read – CHOCOLATIERS & CONFECTIONERS.

Mr. and Mrs. Belmont appeared on the stairs, deep in conversation, and spoke to the man painting the letters. 'I'm sorry George, but we still haven't agreed on the name for our café, and I know you are needing to get on. We'll try and give you the answer tomorrow and then you can make the sign for the front.'

Later that evening, having yet again scared the living daylights out of another of Mr. Menzies' assistants, who looked so shocked she thought he was going to faint, Betty drifted through the wall to take a peak at the attic bakery. She thought everyone had gone home, but the lights were lit and Mr. Belmont (or 'darling Dickie' as Mrs. Belmont called him), was bent over the marble table decorating a large cake with icing. He looked wonderful, she thought, in a crisp white uniform, high collar and long apron. His tall hat almost brushed the ceiling (he was quite a tall man). He had an air of deep concentration as he spread the icing perfectly smooth. He piped rows of shells around the edge and a lattice of fine, evenly spaced lines around the sides, before adding a filigree of white icing fans that stood up like starched lace. Finally, in the palest pink icing he wrote the words 'Welcome To'.

But then he stopped, piping bag held in mid air and stood stock still, frowning. After a moment he put the bag down with an exasperated grunt, took off his apron, turned off the lights and descended down the stairs. Betty heard the faint sound of the front door click shut a few moments later, and then silence.

She looked at the cake and experienced a strong feeling of longing. How she would have loved to have been a confectioner. Perhaps if that carriage hadn't knocked her down when she was only 15 she might have had a chance. The Prospect Hotel was quite posh (although not as posh as The Old Swan of course) and they often had very distinguished clientele up from London to take the spa waters. Once they even had a member of the royal family, though she wasn't allowed to do those rooms, or even look at Her Highness, but she did take a peep when the housekeeper wasn't looking. She thought she wouldn't be a chambermaid forever, but might one day be allowed to serve in the dining room.

But to be able to decorate cakes like this one... that would be a real privilege. She picked up the piping bag and squeezed it gently. Nothing happened. She squeezed a bit harder and jumped when a long wiggle of icing suddenly squirted out, all over the tabletop. She tried again and this time managed to make a slightly wobbly circle shape, which she found very pleasing. Although Betty couldn't write many words, she could

write her name quite elegantly. She had practised lots
of times making the 'B' deliciously fat and round, and
adding a swooping tail to the 'y'. In fact Betty loved
seeing her name written down. Holding the icing
bag carefully, she wrote her name several times on
the marble, each time becoming more confident. She
imagined what it would be like to be one of those
lovely waitresses, serving the Harrogate ladies with
dainty cakes and silver pots of tea. She imagined how
it would be if she owned the café. She would call it
'Bettys Café'. With the last of the icing she filled in the
blank space on the cake and stood back to admire her
work. It said, 'Welcome To Bettys'.

'There, Mr. Belmont!' she thought with satisfaction,
and floated off through the wall into number 11 to
curl up in the wardrobe of the children's bedroom for a
well-earned rest.

At five o'clock the next morning, Frederick
Belmont arrived in the attic bakery, put on his apron,
and stared in astonishment at the cake.

'I don't remember writing that last night,' he
thought, 'but I must have. It's certainly my handiwork. I
wonder why I wrote Bettys?' He shrugged. 'Well, that's

it then. But I'll never be able to explain why I chose that name. I'll just have to say "it's a mystery" because that will certainly be the truth!'

★ 'My Swiss Café' and 'fresh and dainty'

This story arrived in a large crumpled brown envelope, pushed under the front door by an unseen hand. The author must have their own reasons for remaining anonymous, but thank you for your contribution, whoever you are.

JILLY COOPER

Betty was a Yorkshire lass

Full of dreams and oozing class.

Ambition never let her rest

Till everything she made was best.

Now her name is known worldwide

An enduring source of Yorkshire pride.

"A toast to Betty"

Jilly Cooper's first big novel, Riders, was published in 1985 and went straight to number one in the best-seller lists. This was just the start of her great success as an author, which has seen her sell over 11 million copies of her books in the UK alone and have her work translated to be enjoyed around the world. Jilly was appointed OBE in 2004 for services to literature.

PHILIPPA GREGORY

The young man kissed her gloved hands; started to pull off her new kid-skin gloves.

'Don't,' she said. 'Stop it Frederick. People will stare.'

'We're going to open a great restaurant,' he said. 'A wonderful place just like the great cafés at my home in Switzerland, and we will make our fortune, and I shall make you so 'appy, the 'appiest woman in 'orkshire.'

'Yorkshire,' she corrected him but she loved his accent.

The train hooted, the steam engulfed them. 'You will have to tell the sign maker the name!' she called as he leaned from the train window, reaching for her. 'And I am not kissing you in public!'

He laughed and pulled up the leather strap to close the window, blowing kisses to her instead. But he did not forget to telephone the sign maker when he changed trains at York and went into the little call box with his pennies.

The line was bad, the station was noisy, an engine whistled as the old Yorkshire man came to the phone.

'It is to be called Petit Suisse!' Frederick Belmont told him.

'Say again, lad.'

'Petit Suisse! Petit Suisse! For my homeland, Little Switzerland.'

'Oh aye,' said George. He put down the telephone and made a note so that he would not forget.

'Did you hear him right?' his wife asked. 'I thought he wanted to call it 'Something café?'

'Clear as a bell. It's a teashop isn't it? Bettys Teas.'

Philippa Gregory is a writer, historian and broadcaster. Her interest in the Tudor period inspired her to write a number of novels including the international best-seller, The Other Boleyn Girl *which was made into a TV drama and a major film.*

Neil Hanson

She was just seventeen when the war broke out –
the Great War as we came to know it – and she got
engaged to her childhood sweetheart, Ernie, the same
day that he told her he'd enlisted and was going away
to war. Ernie was in one of the 'Pals' regiments that
went 'over the top' at the Battle of the Somme and was
so badly wounded that he lost his right arm, though he
always brushed away any sympathy. 'I was one of the
fortunate ones, son,' he said to me once. 'I survived'.

However, he was captured by the Germans and

held in a prison camp near Hanover for the rest of the war. The food they were given was terrible and grew steadily worse as the war went on. All they had was 'ersatz' coffee, made from dried acorns or burnt barley, black bread so old and stale you could break a tooth on it – some prisoners even used it for fuel – and so-called soup made from water and mangolds or the dried peel of turnips. What kept them alive were the food parcels sent from their families at home and the Red Cross.

As soon as she discovered that Ernie was a prisoner of war, Betty put on her apron and started baking. For the rest of the war Ernie received a parcel every other day, full of home-baked bread and the most delicious scones, cakes and biscuits he'd ever tasted. He shared them with his comrades and before long Betty was baking for them too. My aunt said that at times, it seemed like Betty was baking for the whole British army! She learned how to roast coffee beans too and sent Ernie a regular supply. I still treasure a photograph my aunt took of Betty in her starched white apron, her face pink from the heat of the oven and her hands still dusty with flour, but almost hidden from view by the mounds of cakes and fresh-baked biscuits surrounding her; even now it makes my mouth water just to look at it.

When Ernie came home at the end of the war they got married in their local church – no prizes for guessing who baked and iced the cake for the reception – set up home together and before long a daughter, my mother, came along. However, job prospects for a man with only one arm were bleak and Betty had to work the night-shift at a textile mill just to make ends meet. One day Ernie said to her 'You know what Betty? You make the most wonderful bread and cakes. Why don't you give up the textile job and open a café instead?'

She did. And you know the rest of the story, don't you?

Neil Hanson is the author of an acclaimed series of popular histories including The Custom of the Sea, The Confident Hope of a Miracle *and* The Unknown Soldier. *He has also written as a ghost-writer on behalf of a treasure diver, a polar explorer, two fast-jet pilots and half a dozen SAS men among many others.*

JOANNE HARRIS

Very few people know this, but the genius behind
Bettys tea-shop wasn't really a woman at all. She
wasn't even a baker. In fact, she was a small boy by the
name of Charlie Finn, who lived on the back-streets
of Harrogate and looked after horses for a living.
Charlie's Dad was a farrier. His mother was just a
memory. And ever since he could remember, Charlie
had worked as a farrier's boy, cleaning out stables,
leading horses, helping his father shoe the brutes, in
the expectation that when he grew up, he too might

be a farrier. But Charlie had a secret. He'd always hated horses. The horses hated him too, and never missed the opportunity to give Charlie a kick or a bite.

Mr Finn was at a loss. 'Whatever will come of you, boy?' he used to say to his hapless son. 'Whoever heard of a farrier who was afraid of horses?'

But at twelve years old, Charlie knew what he really wanted to do. He wanted to be a baker. His local baker was called Mr Bettison, and he was well known throughout Yorkshire as the worst baker in the county. His loaves were hard, his biscuits were soft and his cakes were heavy as puddings. To be fair to Mr Bettison, this wasn't entirely his fault. He was a widower, and most of the work in the bakery was done by his daughter Matilda, who was good for nothing, he said, but talk, talk, talk. She couldn't clean, she couldn't sew and definitely couldn't bake. She spent most of her day talking to tradesmen and the rest of the day in helpless tears, crying over burnt biscuits, hard bread and cakes that just refused to rise.

One day, when her father had showed himself especially impatient over a batch of scones that might have served as cobblestones, a horse passing in the street lost a shoe outside the shop, throwing its rider to the ground.

Matilda came out to see what was wrong just as Charlie Finn and his father arrived on the scene. Charlie was trying to calm the horse, a rather bad-tempered young grey, and hoping it wouldn't bite him. He was making a rotten job of it too; and Matilda who was fourteen and had always loved horses, stepped in and took the bridle.

In moments, as if by magic, the horse was calm enough to shoe, and Charlie, whose curiosity had been aroused by the smell from inside the baker's shop, had gone inside to investigate. He saw the sad little pile of scones and the new batch of pastry that Matilda had left on the table, and with the instinct of all things baked, he saw where she was going wrong. Without pausing to measure the quantities he added to the pastry some raisins, some cherries, some sugar, some lard and some secret ingredients of his own that to this day no-one but Bettys bakers know. By the time Matilda's father came in, young Charlie had invented the confection now known as the Yorkshire Fat Rascal, and Matilda had talked her way into a new job with the horse's owner, a gentleman who kept thirty horses in his stables, and who knew raw talent when he saw it.

After that Charlie stayed at Bettison's, which soon came to be known as Bettys, and which earned itself the reputation of being the finest baker's in Yorkshire — some say, in all the Empire.

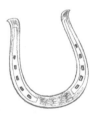

French-British author, Joanne Harris, was born in South Yorkshire. She was a teacher for fifteen years, during which time she published her first novels, including the world-famous, Chocolat, *which was made into an Oscar-nominated film. Joanne's books are now published in over 40 countries and have won a number of British and international awards.*

Blimey... this will throw a
Works

anner in the

TONY HUSBAND

Tony Husband's cartoons have been enjoyed across Britain, appearing in newspapers and magazines, including The Times, Punch and The Sun, as well as in several TV and theatrical productions. His work has won more than 15 major awards and Yobs, which he draws for Private Eye, is one of the best-known comic-strips in Britain.

IAN McMILLAN

I thought I caught a misty glimpse of her the other
shimmering morning as I walked towards the sea: there
she was, in a bright kitchen, bending low over a table,
making pastry.

Then I thought I saw her on the beach, by an oven
made of sand, baking bread that made the seagulls swirl.

Then I saw her walking in the village, clutching a
recipe close to her chest as though it was a secret.
And maybe it was: the writing was small, and intricate.

She was in the crowded market, list in hand,

selecting ingredients that shone and sparkled
and danced.

She sat alone in the enormous Library of Food,
studying the forgotten food masterpieces of Ilkley,
York, Harrogate, Northallerton.

I thought I saw her in the steam of a bakery's back
room, holding aloft some sculpted delight fashioned
with currants and candied peel.

I thought I heard her singing as she mixed mixture
in a mixture-filled mixing bowl that shone in the
afternoon sun.

I dreamed about her and in my dream she was
everywhere in Yorkshire and beyond, and the flour on
her fingers was turning to gold. And the sultanas were
jewels: rubies, diamonds, cherries.

And then I woke up and ate a Fat Rascal.

Known as The Bard of Barnsley, *Ian McMillan is a well-loved poet,
broadcaster, commentator and programme maker. Aside from his many
volumes of poetry for adults and children, Ian presents* The Verb *every
week on BBC Radio 3 and tours the country with* The Ian McMillan
Orchestra.

KAY MELLOR

Frederick, a talented young Swiss confectioner, had journeyed to England to capitalise on his culinary skills and open a café in London.

On a cold November night in 1919 he asked a porter in his best English which train he should catch for Haringey. The porter, thinking he'd said Harrogate, pointed him in the direction of the steam train heading for Yorkshire. The carriage was cold and the air was damp, which didn't help the cough that he'd recently developed. The journey took six and a half hours and by the time Frederick stepped off the train into a dimly lit railway station, a fever was raging through his body. He looked about for anyone who might help him with his trunk as he felt quite weak, but there was nobody in sight. Then his eyes fell upon a young woman who was sitting on a nearby bench. She was looking down at her hands, which were on her lap. Thinking she might be able to help, he headed over to her.

'Excuse me Mademoiselle; do you know if in this station there might be a servant or porter who could…?'

The young woman looked up and Frederick could see that her face was stained with tears. The shy young woman's face was the last image Frederick saw before he woke up in the station tea room.

'Where am I?' Frederick stammered in his native tongue as he looked about the tea room. The young girl offered him some sweet tea.

'Harrogate Station tea room. Drink this Sir and you'll feel better.'

'Is he coming round?' asked Alice, the common-looking tea lady, as she peered over the counter.

'I think so,' answered the shy girl.

Frederick sipped the sweet tea. He wasn't sure if he liked it, but it warmed his body and made him feel strangely comforted. He looked around and realised customers with curious-looking pots and jugs on their tables were all staring at him as they sipped from their tea cups. He'd heard about the English custom of tea drinking, but this was the first time he'd seen it with his own eyes.

The Station Master entered. He was a middle-aged, portly man with bushy grey eyebrows and a ruddy complexion.

'Do you have any brass lad?!' he bellowed.

Frederick didn't understand his strong Yorkshire accent.

'Money,' the shy young girl explained.

Frederick told them he had plenty of money, just neither the good health nor the stamina to lift his trunk.

The Station Master told him he could 'sort out an 'orse and cart and get his stuff shifted.'

The young girl translated and helped Frederick look for the piece of paper with the address of where he was supposed to be going written on it.

Realising the man was wealthy and thinking he might earn himself a generous tip, the Station Master raced off to find a hansom cab or cart. Meanwhile, the young girl sat with Frederick and he managed to make some conversation with her. He established her name was Elizabeth Braithwaite, but everyone called her Betty. Frederick asked why she was so upset; he could see that she had been crying. After some hesitation she explained how she was supposed to be catching the 8.30pm train back to Northumberland where she worked in service as a kitchen maid; however, she'd let the train pull out of the station because she was worried about her family. Her father had been killed in a farming accident five months ago and her mother had been inconsolable. She was finding life difficult and wasn't coping with her two young sons and baby daughter. Betty told Frederick she had spent the whole weekend cleaning the house and baking for the children. Frederick was intrigued, what did she bake? Betty told him she made many things and she offered Frederick a buttered scone that she'd packed up for her journey back to Northumberland. Realising he hadn't eaten anything for at least eight hours, he thanked her and sank his teeth into the soft scone.

Frederick was transfixed by the scone and its unique taste. It was sweet, yet savoury, light, but with dried fruit. In short, it was utterly delicious. He'd worked in confectionery all his life but he'd never tasted anything quite like it.

The Station Master bustled back into the tea room, his face redder than ever and a thin film of sweat forming on his brow.

'I've got yer an 'orse and carriage, but yer've come to the wrong place lad. This is Harrogate, not Haringey what's written on this here piece of paper. Yer were nowt but a cough and a spit from Haringey afore yer got on the bloomin' train lad, Haringey's in London!'

Frederick couldn't believe he had made such a mistake. Maybe his brain had been clouded through fever and fatigue. He felt somewhat revived by the sweet tea and scone, but clearly was in no fit state to travel. Betty told him he'd be welcome to stay with her family, he could sleep in her bed and she would climb in with her mother. Frederick was overcome with Betty's generosity. He gave the Station Master a generous tip and Betty helped him out of the railway station to the awaiting hansom cab.

It was a long bumpy ride back to where Betty lived and Frederick coughed and winced as the carriage sped along the country roads heading six miles north of Harrogate. Frederick's pallor became pale and sallow as the journey progressed. Betty became concerned for his health as he looked as though he was about to faint again. She asked the driver to stop by a nearby stream, dipped her scarf in the cool water and mopped Frederick's brow to try and bring his temperature down. Frederick took hold of Betty's hand.

'I can never thank you enough little Betty, you are my saviour.'

Betty thought nothing of it; it was her nature to help.

Once they'd arrived at her home, Betty showed Frederick to his room and then she quietly climbed into bed next to her mother, taking care not to wake the baby. The next morning Betty woke to find her two young brothers bouncing excitedly on the bed.

'Betty's come back!!!' they yelped.

Betty's gaunt-faced mother, Ida, appeared in the doorway.

'What are you doing home and who is the stranger in your bed?'

Betty told her mother what had happened and begged her to let the man stay just for a few days till he was strong enough to travel back to London. She told her mother she was going to give in her notice at Rutherford House and try and find some work locally. Ida was relieved to have her daughter home, but worried how they would manage as they relied totally on Betty's wage to live. The cottage was tied to her late husband's job and the farmer had already told her she was going to have to leave by the end of the month.

Frederick stayed at the cottage for nearly three weeks. He enjoyed the warmth and hospitality of Betty's family and got to sample more Yorkshire culinary delights – jam tarts, curd tarts and butterfly buns. Frederick realised that Betty had learnt her baking skills from her mother and would often compliment both mother and daughter. Ida enjoyed having a man about the house. She would sometimes take the baby for a walk in her pram and Frederick would accompany her. She would tell him all her worries and recall tales of how she met her husband

and how happy they were together. He told her about his life back in Switzerland and how the Yorkshire countryside air reminded him of the clean air of his native Alps. Slowly Frederick's cough got better and Ida's depression began to lift.

Betty had baked a fresh loaf of bread and picked some wild bilberries, sweetening them with sugar, and made them into a pie for their last supper together.

Frederick scraped his bowl clean, put his spoon down and said he had something to tell them.

Ida told the boys to be quiet.

Frederick cleared his throat, took a drink of the sweet elderflower water Betty had poured for him and began in his broken English –

'Over the last three weeks I have spent here with you, I have been supremely happy and for that I thank you from the bottom, top and in fact all of my heart. I think of you as my friends and you have made me think differently about what I am to do....'

All eyes were on Frederick.

'I have decided after all of this, not to return to London.'

Both Betty and Ida were delighted as they'd grown fond of Frederick. The boys jumped up and down and hugged Frederick, which brought tears to his eyes.

'Fate has brought me to Harrogate, and this is where I intend to stay; and furthermore.... I am going to open a tea room, the best tea room in Harrogate and I am going to sell amongst other things Betty's scones, breads and pies.'

Betty's and Ida's eyes were as large as saucers, the boys squealed and danced about the room and the baby giggled.

'You will make them for me, for my tea room, and I shall pay you handsomely. In fact I will give you one hundred pounds now to ensure your service.'

Both Betty and her mother were astounded – one hundred pounds! They couldn't even imagine that much money.

'There is only one condition,' Frederick said, 'that I have your permission to call my tea room Bettys. And I hope that all who work there extend the same generosity, kindness and hospitality to others that you and your wonderful family have shown to me.'

Tears of happiness trickled down Betty's face as she

hugged her mother and little brothers – their future was secured.

Betty and Ida also helped Frederick choose the location and building for the tea room. They helped him choose the tables and chairs, the decorations, the colour of the paint, the crockery, the linen and the menu.

The day before the grand opening, Frederick took Betty and her family to see the tea room. They stood across the road gazing up at the impressive-looking building with its burgundy sweeping signage proudly bearing the name 'Bettys'. Frederick asked Betty if she approved of the sign. She blushed and told him she didn't realise the sign would be so big and on the high street where everyone could see it. Frederick told her that if it was her wish, he wouldn't tell anyone who Betty was – it would be their secret. Amongst the staff she would be known as Elizabeth. Betty felt reassured.

Within six months Betty and Ida had to enlist the help of two girls from the village to meet the orders. Within eighteen months they had moved out of rented accommodation and bought a family house in Harrogate.

Although Frederick never revealed the inspiration behind the name of the tea room to another soul, he would often smile as he looked up at the sign and remember with great tenderness that cold November night back in 1919, when an act of human kindness led to what would one day become one of Yorkshire's greatest assets.

One of the UK's most successful television drama writers, Kay Mellor still lives in Leeds where she was born. She has written continuously for theatre and television, and her shows over the years, including Band of Gold *and* Fat Friends, *have won and been nominated for numerous awards. Kay was appointed OBE for services to drama in 2009.*

MIKE PANNETT

It was quiz night at the Jolly Farmers. PC Mike
Pannett was chewing his pencil. Soapy drained the last
drop of beer from his pint pot and shoved it hopefully
towards Algy. Surely it was his round. But Algy was
deep in thought. This tie-break question was a poser,
and no mistake. But old Walter was looking serenely
confident. He was on top of his game tonight. It was
thanks to him the team were still in with a shout.

'Right lads,' Ann said, picking up the answer sheet.

'Have we decided? Bettys tea rooms. Who's it named after?'

Mike shrugged and slung his pencil onto the table. 'Haven't a clue. Unless it was their canteen dinner lady.'

'Soapy?'

'Aye, Mike could be onto sommat there. A canteen lady. That's just the sort of name they had. Madge, Elsie, Betty.... Mind, I knew a Betty one time. Lovely lass. Wanted to marry me, but....' He shook his head. 'Clueless. Couldn't bake for toffee. And when she mashed me a cuppa tea, why, it were like warmed up pond water.'

'We'll take that as a "don't know",' Ann said, and turned to Algy. 'How about you?'

'Bit of a teaser, isn't it?' He rubbed his chin. History was his subject, so he ought to be able to come up with something. 'D'you know, somewhere at the back of my mind I've a dim recollection of a young lady – '

'I bet you have, cock-bod.'

'Quite so, Soapy, quite so. Yes, Betty Lupton was her name and I believe she was responsible for ladling out the spa waters at Harrogate. They called her "The Queen of Harrogate Wells".'

'That makes sense,' said Mike. 'Harrogate? I mean, it's Bettys head office, isn't it? Case closed, I'd say.'

But Algy looked doubtful. 'Mind, I'm going back two hundred years now. Late eighteenth century, so the evidence is a bit sketchy.'

'Maybe the answer's staring us in the face,' Ann cut in.

'What do you mean?'

'Well, who was the founder's wife?'

'Elizabeth, wasn't it?'

'And short for Elizabeth is…?'

'Ah, Betty. Good one,' Mike said. 'But if it was that easy it wouldn't be such a mystery.'

'This is all frightfully interesting,' Algy said. 'If I'm not mistaken the name Elizabeth has something to do with "God" or "God's promise".'

'Well, as I like to remind everyone whenever I get the chance, we are in God's Own County,' Mike said. 'Perhaps that's who Betty is: our wonderful county of Yorkshire.'

'Why, you're blooming clueless,' Walt could contain himself no longer. 'The lot of you. The answer's staring you right in t'face.'

'Go on then, Walt. Let's hear it.'

'Up on t'moors there, above Rosedale Head.'

Algy frowned. 'I'm awfully sorry but I'm none the wiser, old chap.'

'I'm talking about them stone crosses.'

'Aye, I know the ones,' Soapy said. 'There's a whole load of 'em. Used to show travellers the way, didn't they?'

'I still don't get it,' Mike said. 'What's a stone cross got to do with it?'

Walt tutted, and shoved his empty glass towards Algy. 'I thought you knew your way around your patch, lad. You want to get yourself up top end of Rosedale. You'll see. There's a little low stumpy one wi' a white painted cross.'

'Oh… now that you mention it,' Mike started.

'Aye, the penny drops – at blooming last. Now then, lad, what do they call her?'

'Ah!' Algy clicked his fingers. 'Of course. Fat Betty. I remember it now. Went for a school outing up there, years ago, when I was still in short trousers. We all sat

[66]

round it and ate salmon and cucumber sandwiches, washed down with a flask of hot tea.'

'Afternoon tea with Fat Betty?' Mike laughed. 'I like it.'

'We all agreed, then?' Ann had her pencil poised over the answer sheet.

'Aye,' said Soapy. 'Get it put down, lass. Then maybe Algy can get his round in – before we perish.'

Yorkshire born and bred, Mike Pannett is known for his tales of a Yorkshire Bobby. He has written several best-selling books, which are inspired by his time as a rural beat officer with the North Yorkshire police. His latest book, Just The Job Lad *was recently released. Mike served for nearly twenty years in the police force, during which time he became one of the highest commended officers. In 2010 he became a 'Patron of Yorkshire'.*

GERVASE PHINN

Few people might be aware that the very first Bettys was originally destined to be Rotherham's (and not Harrogate's) premier tea room and café. Perhaps I should explain.

Frederick Belmont, an idealistic and ambitious young Swiss confectioner, arrived in London intent on starting his own business. English tea rooms at the time were largely unimaginative places which served insipid ham sandwiches, hard rock buns, sickly sweet cream cakes and watery tea. Here was a real business opportunity for the talented and enterprising confectioner. London was his first choice to start a café tea room, but being new to the country and unable to understand the porter at the London station, young Frederick by mistake took the train bound for Yorkshire. This was just after the First World War and anti-German feeling was high, so when one of Frederick's fellow passengers heard the young man speaking to the guard in a pronounced German accent, he began berating him. Frederick attempted to explain that he was, in fact, Swiss and not German, but to no avail and the atmosphere in the carriage became more heated when another passenger voiced his strong disapproval of the presence in the carriage of 'the German foreigner'. Frederick felt it politic to leave and disembarked at the next station, which was Sheffield. Unfortunately for him one of the obstreperous passengers also alighted at Sheffield and continued to shout and curse and cause a most unpleasant scene on the platform. The police were called.

My great-grandfather, Michael Touhy, PC E56 in the Sheffield Police Force, was called to deal with the fracas. He calmed things down and took the distressed young Swiss confectioner for a cup of tea, assuring him that Yorkshire people were not like the angry southerners who had verbally attacked him, but were the friendliest folk in the country. It was getting dark and the young man had nowhere to stay so my great-grandfather, who was coming off duty within the hour, suggested that Frederick might like to accompany him home to the small red-brick terrace and spend the night there with the Touhy family. Here Frederick met my great-aunt Betty, Michael Touhy's younger and strikingly beautiful sister. Her real name was Elizabeth Anne Mary Touhy but in the family she was called Betty. The young Frederick was made more than welcome and stayed for several weeks enjoying the hospitality of the Touhys. Being an industrious young man he took on much of the cooking and supplemented the family's diet of soda bread, cabbage and potatoes with his wonderful confections: rich fruitcakes and light sponges, chocolate roulade and curd tarts, delicious buns and Swiss rolls, apple pies and cream hearts, all freshly made from proper ingredients. Such was the quality of the produce that word spread and people began calling to purchase his confections. My great-aunt persuaded young Frederick to set up a stall on Rotherham Market (originally called 'Fred's Fancies') and every Saturday people queued for the crusty bread and delicious cakes, pastries and chocolates.

When a modest property became available near the great red sandstone parish church of All Saints' in the centre of Rotherham, it was decided Frederick would purchase the premises and realise his dream. It would be called 'The Ring O' Bells Café and Tea Room' and be managed by Betty. It was assumed in the family that she would become Mrs Belmont within the year, for the couple were clearly very much in love. Sadly, this was not to be for Betty, hurrying across Corporation Street one icy winter day, slipped and was killed by the oncoming Middlewood tram. Heartbroken, Frederick took the train north and ended up in Harrogate vowing that should he ever open a café tea room it would be called after the young woman with the flame-red hair, jade green eyes and dazzling smile. The rest, as they say, is history.

Author and educator Gervase Phinn was born and bred in South Yorkshire. He is best known for his autobiographical Dales *books, which are full of colourful characters – many encountered during his years working as a schools inspector in the Yorkshire Dales, and have become best-sellers.*

MARK REID

As a Harrogate lad (OK, I wasn't born in Harrogate, but my family moved from Lancashire to Harrogate when I was six) I have often pondered who Betty was. As a student, my guitar-playing friend and I used to busk in an alleyway off James Street, and then head off to Bettys after an hour or so to count our takings and treat ourselves to a large cup of Café Blend coffee, paid for with copper coins! We would often ask our waitress who Betty was, but we never found out. But busking in the cold and rain was not good for my saxophone, so I got a job during the summer holidays in the Bettys & Taylors factory packing the freshly ground coffee into bags, still warm from the roaster. But alas, no-one could spill the coffee beans there either as to who Betty was. I then assumed it was Betty Lupton, Harrogate's most famous dispenser of the curative waters during the 19th century.

But then, twenty years later, I thought I had a breakthrough. I had just finished a large cup of Café Blend coffee (it really is rather good) and a Fat Rascal, and my two young children were carefully dabbing up the crumbs from their plates with their fingers when I thought I would ask the waitress one last time.

'Was everything OK for you?' asked the well-presented waitress.

'Fine, thank you,' I replied, and then added nonchalantly 'by the way, who's Betty?'

Without a pause, the waitress replied, 'Oh, she's not in today. Betty works on a Saturday.'

....

Mark Reid is one of the UK's leading experts on country pubs and long distance walks. After moving to North Yorkshire and falling in love with the countryside of the Yorkshire Dales, he was inspired to write the acclaimed Inn Way *and* Walking Weekends *series of walking guide books, which cover all the national parks of Northern England.*

NICHOLAS RHEA

The secret behind the name of Bettys is there for everyone to see in the logo of the tea rooms. There is no apostrophe, which indicates the rooms are not named after one particular Betty, but several. Most are recorded in the various written histories of Bettys Tea Rooms, but one Betty has been overlooked – which is precisely what she intended. Research indicates that the true Betty was well known in the Harrogate/Knaresborough area even though we know so little about her role at Bettys.

First, however, we must recall the known candidates.

No.1: Frederick Belmont, the founder of Bettys, is said to have named his tea rooms after the daughter of the doctor who practised next door to his first café in Cambridge Crescent, Harrogate.

No.2: Betty Lupton famously dispensed the sulphur waters of Harrogate for sixty years from 1778, so who better to give her name to the new Harrogate tea room?

No.3: Around 1915 a London musical show called *Betty* attracted Frederick's attention and he fell for the leading lady whose name was also Betty.

No.4: A pretty child called Betty Rose walked into a room where Frederick and his fellow directors were meeting to decide upon a name for the tea rooms. The girl was carrying a tea-tray and so it was decided to call the tea rooms Betty's in her honour – at that time with the apostrophe.

No.5: Did Frederick actually name the tea-rooms after his bride, Bunny, a beautician and hairdresser whose professional name was Betty?

No.6: Bethany Ridsdale, a Yorkshire woman.

Here are six possible Bettys. So is it a coincidence

that there are six Bettys Tea Rooms? All in Yorkshire?

The question must now be asked – who was Bethany Ridsdale?

The name Betty is a popular diminutive form of Elizabeth. Others include Bess, Bessie, Betsy, Bettina, Bette and Beth. However, Betty is also the diminutive name of Bethany, a name of Biblical origins that used to mean a house of poverty. When Frederick established his first tea rooms in Cambridge Crescent at Harrogate he was far from wealthy although not poverty-stricken, and he could afford to employ a young woman called Bethany Ridsdale.

His Cambridge Crescent premises were known for their long, narrow rooms but Frederick knew he must keep everything scrupulously clean if he was to attract the right clientele, and so he employed a cleaning lady. She was Bethany Ridsdale who also rejoiced in the nickname of Betty Besom.

Besom was a rude word used in Scotland to describe a young woman who was considered rather cheeky, naughty and forward – a feisty lady in fact. However, this was in Yorkshire, not Scotland, and it is not the reason why Bethany Ridsdale was known as

Betty Besom. It was probably the fact she used a besom to sweep the floors of the new tea rooms. A besom was ideal because it was particularly effective at cleaning corners and would also remove leaves that settled on pebbles or un-surfaced roads. By using her besom, therefore, along with other cleaning aids, Bethany kept the tea rooms and their surrounds in an immaculate condition and so Frederick's café soon attracted the fashionable people of the area. Frederick was quick to appreciate Bethany's early role in helping his fledgling business to flourish.

However, apart from the skill with a besom, there was another reason why Bethany was called Betty Besom.

One of her leisure interests was participation in the Knaresborough Plough Stots. The blossoming township of Harrogate was formerly within the ancient and historic Knaresborough Forest. Indeed, a thorn tree from that huge forest continued to thrive for years in Montpellier Gardens near Bettys tea shop on Harrogate's Parliament Street.

The Plough Stots were a team of male folk dancers who, on Plough Monday each year, dressed in colourful costumes and performed elaborate sword-dances in local towns and villages. Plough Monday was normally the first Monday after the Feast of the Epiphany (January 6th), which was traditionally the day when farmhands resumed work after the Christmas and New Year holiday. The word stot means bullock, and when the dancers moved around villages and towns, they knocked on doors to solicit money for charity and if the householders refused, the Stots would threaten to plough a furrow outside their homes.

Even though the Stots were a male dancing group, there was a female character in their performances. She was called Betty Besom. The leading man was known as T'Awd Man and the leading woman was T'Awd Woman. In Knaresborough's case, that female character was Betty Besom and she was always played by Bethany Ridsdale.

The fact that she was widely known by her dancing name but also used a besom during her cleaning jobs, made it inevitable she would be popularly known by that name, as indeed she was when working for Frederick Belmont. In addition to her cleaning duties, she could also act as an efficient and charming waitress, and then Frederick, much to his surprise, discovered she was a most capable baker of exquisite cakes, buns and delicacies.

As his business flourished, he came to depend upon her and so, when he (and Bethany) moved into new premises in Parliament Street (where Bettys tea rooms remain) he wanted to honour her commitment in the name of his enterprise.

But Betty Besom would have none of it.

'I don't want folks to know or even think it's me,' she told Frederick in no uncertain manner. 'Apart from anything else, folks might get the wrong idea.'

'I can understand that but finding the right name for these tea-rooms is extremely important,' Frederick insisted. He was not easily diverted from his chosen path and continued, 'Even if we call the new tea rooms Betty's, very few of our customers will associate it with you, you've always been so very discreet. As you know, other Bettys have been associated with our tea rooms so the name could refer to any of them.'

'Then don't use the apostrophe,' she suggested. 'Without it, it'll be linked to all the Bettys. And I don't want you mentioning me in anything you write about the tea rooms, now or in the future.'

'So if I agree to that, you won't mind me using the name?' he asked tentatively.

'Not at all, Mr Belmont – but remember, no apostrophe. Then nobody will think it's me, will they?'

'Sadly, no,' he admitted but Frederick was a man of his word and never disclosed the source of Bettys name.

Nicholas Rhea lives in North Yorkshire, the county where he first joined the North Yorkshire police force as a beat bobby in Whitby in 1956. In time he began to write about his experiences in policing, and his Constable *stories provided the inspiration for the hugely popular* Heartbeat *TV series, which ran for 18 years and is still enjoyed around the world.*

JACK SHEPHERD

Betty lived in a little terrace house in the middle of Brew Street, on the outskirts of Charborough, Yorkshire. She was quite old. This is what she looked like.

She could remember a time when she had a family around her, and a husband called Arthur, but that was long ago.

Her son Maurice would visit her on alternate Sunday afternoons, and bring his two children with him. Maurice was a manager in a factory that manufactured cloth. He was very short-sighted like his mother, and liked everything done in an orderly fashion.

Betty's best friend was called Maude. She was very kind and often helped Betty with her shopping. Sometimes in the afternoons they would take tea together in Betty's kitchen. Betty would sprinkle a spoonful of tea into Maude's cup. Then she would add boiling water, milk and sugar.

BETTY'S BEST FRIEND MAUDE

In those days tea was always made in a cup. This was before the teapot had been invented. And the tea bag was little more than a twinkle in the eye of its creator.

THE INVENTOR OF THE TEA BAG, DREAMING OF HIS CREATION.

Sometimes in the afternoon the vicar would come round and join Betty and Maude for tea. The problem was that when her friends drank the tea at the very bottom of the cup, it was always too strong, and sometimes the tea leaves would stick together and slide out of the cup and slop onto their laps, and on several occasions the vicar had inadvertently inhaled the tea leaves and started to choke.

THE VICAR GETTING A MOUTHFUL OF TEA.

THE VICAR BEGINS TO CHOKE

The only person who enjoyed Betty's tea was her friend Griselda Pike, who was psychic and enjoyed telling people's fortunes by reading the tea leaves in the cup. So whenever she was having tea at Betty's house, she was very grateful that the tea was *always* full of them.

GRISELDA PIKE

It was Maurice, however, on one of his Sunday afternoon visits, who told her she had to start making tea for people in a QUICKER MORE EFFICIENT way! Simply brewing the tea in the cup JUST WASN'T GOOD ENOUGH. She should try and find a way of brewing tea that wasn't so WASTEFUL! (He had just dropped hot tea leaves down his trousers at the time, which explains his sudden loss of temper).

And so with help from her friend Alice, who was doing a course in pottery at night school, and Fred the plumber, who knew a thing or two about welding, she set about trying to invent something that would brew her tea more effectively.

THE TWO SPOUT SOLUTION

MONOSPOUTS

WATER IN

MILK IN

→ TEA OUT

SUGAR IN

CURVED PIPE TO COOL THE TEA ON ITS WAY OUT.

MOBILE TEA POT

Her early efforts were too complicated. So she then got Alice to make her a series of pots of different shapes and sizes.

SOME OF THE TEA POTS WERE MUCH TOO BIG

AND OTHERS... WERE MUCH TOO SMALL

But none of these were very satisfactory.

Then one day, sitting by the fire, Betty saw her cat trying to swat a fly with her paw. The shape her cat made as she clawed at the fly, gave Betty a new idea.

Perhaps her teapot should look like this?

... PERHAPS HER TEA POT SHOULD LOOK LIKE THIS.

And so the next time her friends came round for tea, she tried out the new teapot. Alice had made it for her at one of her pottery classes, and glazed it with a brown glaze.

Maurice was there with his children and her good friend Maude. And the vicar was there too, with Alice, Fred and Griselda Pike.

EVERYONE WAS THERE GATHERED ROUND THE TABLE MAURICE AND HIS TWO CHILDREN MAUDE ...

The tea came out as a clear liquid, with a good strong taste. And everyone was very happy.

... AND THE VICAR GRISELDA PIKE AND FRED

AND EVERYONE WAS VERY HAPPY.

Apart from Griselda Pike, who because she couldn't find any tea leaves floating in the cups, was unable to tell any fortunes.

ESPECIALLY BETTY

Betty on the other hand was very pleased with herself.

Born in Leeds, Jack Shepherd is an actor, playwright, theatre director and jazz musician. He is perhaps best known for his acting roles, most notably the title role in television detective drama Wycliffe, *but he also has an accomplished writing and directing career, staging several productions at Shakespeare's Globe.*

BARBARA TAYLOR BRADFORD

The atmosphere in Mary Wood's dining room in her Harrogate home was fraught with tension.

There they all were... her two sons, her son-in-law, and the new husband of her niece Claire, Frederick Belmont from Switzerland. They were endeavouring to think of a name for a new business Mary had invested in, and were not having any luck. The right name was elusive. It was young Frederick, a talented Swiss confectioner, who was starting his own business with his wife and Mary's financial backing. Ambitious, driven and talented, Frederick was clever at finding names for his many delicious confections, but like the others at the meeting, he could not find the perfect name for his Tea Room and Bakery.

'What about the Swiss Tea Room?' one of Mary's sons suggested. 'It's simple. People will remember it.'

'Too prosaic, and far too simple,' Mary pronounced in her blunt Yorkshire way. 'But Mother, Swiss confectionery is mouth-watering,' another son pointed out. 'And I second the name.' Mary shook her head, but then looked across at her nephew-in-law. After all, it was actually his talent she was backing and banking on. 'What do you think, Frederick?'

'I agree with you, Mary, it is... dull.'

'Quite right. It doesn't work. We need something warm, inviting, personal. A name everyone can identify with.' At this moment, much to their collective surprise, the dining room door swung open and another person walked into their meeting, an uninvited person. They all stared at her. Frederick was particularly startled. He had never seen anyone quite as beautiful as this lovely creature walking toward the table. She was delicately made, delicious looking, positively delectable. Just like a piece of Swiss confectionery, he thought, and smiled to himself at this analogy. She had a peaches-and-cream complexion, exquisite features and silky brown hair touched with golden streaks.

She smiled at Frederick and he smiled back, completely taken with her. Slowly, she came towards him, carrying a tray on which there was a yellow teapot and a matching cup and saucer. He couldn't take his eyes off her as she placed her tray on the table in front of him, and then did a little curtsy. 'Thank you,' he said. 'I'm Frederick Belmont.'

'My name is Winifred Elizabeth Rose,' she answered with another dimpled smile. 'But I'm called Betty Rose.'

'That's it!' Mary Wood exclaimed at once, staring at Frederick. 'I've just had a brainstorm. Let's call it Bettys.'

The four men looked at each other, then they all nodded in agreement. It sounded right to them.

Once the meeting was over, Frederick rushed home to his wife, bursting to give her this important news. 'I fell in love with a beautiful girl today!' he told Claire in an excited voice. 'A delicious-looking girl.'

Claire gaped at him in disbelief. 'F-f-ell in love?' she stammered, looking crestfallen and hurt.

Realising his mistake at once, Frederick hurried over to Claire, and put his arm around her, explained, 'I didn't mean that the way you think. She is only <u>twelve</u>, and she's Aunt Mary's granddaughter. You know her. Her name is Winifred Elizabeth Rose, and we're going to call the tea room after her.'

Recovering herself, now understanding everything, Claire smiled at her young husband, then instantly frowned, her expression one of total perplexity. 'You're going to call the tea room by three names? Winifred Elizabeth Rose? It's a bit long, isn't it?'

'No, it isn't because we're going to call it simply... Bettys. It's warm and welcoming, and people will say let's go to Bettys, and they will feel as if they are going to someone's house for tea.'

And so it was. And still is. And always will be. Simply... Bettys.

Barbara Taylor Bradford started her writing career on the Yorkshire Evening Post. *Her first novel,* A Woman of Substance, *became an enduring best-seller and her books have now sold more than eighty-three million copies in more than ninety countries. Barbara was appointed OBE for her contributions to literature in 2007.*

ALAN TITCHMARSH

It is a little-known fact that Betty was my mother. She baked the most wonderful cakes and scones, brewed a fine cup of tea and smiled sweetly at all she served. The trouble is, her real name was Bessie.

She hated it; said it was only ever given to cows and fire engines. As a result she cajoled the local sign writer into adjusting the name over the shop to 'Bettys' rather than 'Bessies'.

My mother is not to be confused with the auntie who makes Yorkshire puddings (even though Mum's inflated creations were the first in the country). Her speciality was a large bun, studded with cherries, peel and other such treats. She wanted to call it after me, but I was very small and thin as a nipper. 'Wiry rascal' just didn't have the right ring to it. As a result of which she called it after a partly distant cousin whom I never liked.

But I do like going into her tea shop and eating them...

Ah well... a chap can but dream.

But my mum really was called Bessie.

Even if she would have preferred Betty.

Born on the edge of Ilkley Moor, Alan Titchmarsh began working as an apprentice gardener at the age of 15, and has gone on to become one of Britain's most well-known and best-loved gardeners. As well as Alan's TV accolades including the hugely successful Ground Force, *Alan has written over 50 gardening books and a number of best-selling novels. Alan was appointed MBE for services to horticulture and broadcasting in 2000.*